## AUTHOR ID

**Name:** Tony Bradman

**Likes:** Playing football with my grandchildren

**Dislikes:** Being worn out after playing football with my grandchildren

**3 words that best describe me:**
Short, domestic, funny (well my wife says so anyway!)

**A secret not many people know:**
I once played football against a team captained by the England manager's son – and my team won!

## ILLUSTRATOR ID

**Name:** Karen Donnelly

**Likes:** Reading in bed

**Dislikes:** Alarm clocks

**3 words that best describe me:**
Very nice indeed

**A secret not many people know:**
I'm 400 years old – only joking!

For Oscar – the best footballer I know

# One-Nil

by

Tony Bradman

Illustrated by Karen Donnelly

You do not need to read this page – just get on with the book!

First published in 2008 in Great Britain by
Barrington Stoke Ltd
18 Walker St, Edinburgh, EH3 7LP

www.barringtonstoke.co.uk

ISBN: 978-1-84299-518-1

Printed in Great Britain by Bell & Bain Ltd

# Contents

# Chapter 1
# Secret Training

"You're kidding," said Luke. "You must be joking!"

"I'm not," said Jamie. "My dad said the full England squad are training at the City ground tomorrow morning."

*Jamie's dad should know*, thought Luke. After all, his job was looking after the pitch at City, the local club. He was the chief groundsman. Jamie and Luke were best mates, and they were both in their school's football team. Luke had often gone to City with Jamie. Jamie could get in any time because his dad worked there.

Luke and Jamie were on their way home from school. When they got to the gates of the local park, they stopped. Most afternoons they had a kickabout there. But today they went over to the playground and sat on the roundabout instead.

"My dad says no one's meant to know. It's a big secret," said Jamie.

"They must want to practise some set-piece moves without anyone seeing them," said Luke. "It's the big match next week, isn't it?"

England were due to play France in a World Cup game.

"Plus my dad says I can have the day off to go down and watch them train," said Jamie. "Do you want to come too?"

Luke closed his eyes. The roundabout was going round, and he dreamed he was standing on the centre spot in a great stadium. He was turning so he could wave to the crowd. He couldn't think of anything he'd rather do than watch England training – unless it was to pull on a real England shirt, trot out onto the pitch and score a goal. In his mind he saw his hero Steve Browning crossing the ball, he heard the crowd roaring ...

"But I bet your mum won't let you have the day off," said Jamie.

Luke opened his eyes. Jamie was right. He knew it wasn't even worth asking his mum. She didn't like football, or think it was important. And when it came to having time

off school, she was very strict. She got cross if she thought Luke was trying it on.

Luke felt really fed up. The England squad – including Steve Browning – were going to be so close. But they might as well be on the moon for all the good it would do him.

Then suddenly he had an idea.

"I'll be there, Jamie," he said. "I'm not missing out on this."

There was one thing that might make his mum let him stay away from school. But it would need very careful planning ...

# Chapter 2
# A Brilliant Plan

Luke's mum was standing beside his bed, looking down at him.

"Are you sure you don't feel well?" she said.

It was the next morning, and Luke hadn't got out of bed. He looked up at his mum from his bed. He had to make her think that he was ill. Then she'd go off to work and he'd be free to do what he wanted.

"I feel rough, Mum, honest I do," he said. That sounded all right – weak, in pain – but not too much.

Mum sat down on the side of the bed and put her hand on his head. He could feel the cold metal of her wedding ring on his skin.

"You do feel as if you've got a bit of a temperature," she said, and peered into his eyes. "There's a nasty bug going round as well …"

"I won't miss much at school," said Luke. "We've got PE this afternoon and Mr Castle will probably make us do it outside, even if it rains."

"Right, that settles it," said Mum. Luke tried hard not to grin. "You don't want to be running about outside in the cold and wet. Not in your state. The only trouble is – who's going to look after you? I can't take any time off work, and your sister won't be back from

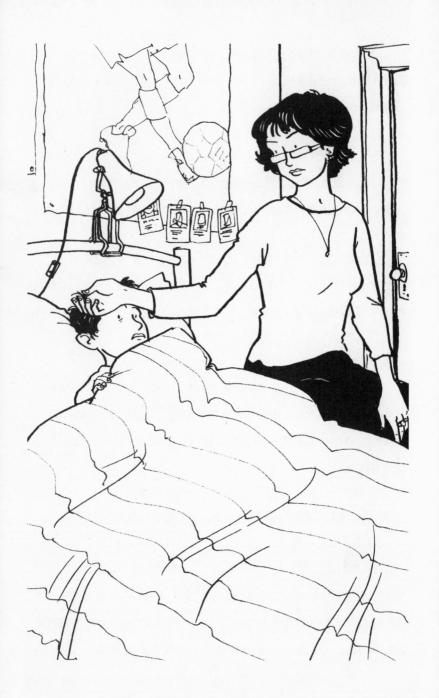

school till this afternoon ..." She stopped talking so as to think about it. "I know, I'll ask Penny – she owes me a favour. I babysat little Tom for her twice last week."

"That's fine by me, Mum," said Luke, remembering to cough.

"Right, I'll ring her now," said Mum, getting to her feet. "You'll be OK on your own for half an hour. It will take her that long to get here. I'll take you to the doctor's tonight if you're no better."

Luke didn't get out of bed until he heard Mum's car turn the corner and go down the main road. He was definitely grinning now. His plan was working. All he had to do was phone Mum's friend Penny and stop her coming. And he knew exactly how he was going to do that, too.

He'd thought about it all yesterday evening. He'd even remembered to check that

Penny's phone number was written in the address book Mum kept by the phone. And he'd worked out what he was going to say ...

"Oh, hello, Luke," Penny said when he rang her. "I'm sorry to hear you're not feeling well. I'll be with you as soon as I –"

"It's OK, you don't have to come now," Luke said quickly. "Mum forgot, my sister's got study leave today. She just has to pop into school to pick up some books. She'll be back to look after me in a little while."

"Well, if you're sure," said Penny. "I don't mind dropping in."

"No, we'll be fine, thanks," said Luke. "And I phoned Mum on her mobile, so you don't need to tell her, either."

"OK then," said Penny. "Hope you feel better soon ... bye!"

Luke put the phone down and stood there with his fists clenched, his eyes closed, and his mind full of football scenes. He was scoring goals for England, he was taking a cross from Steve Browning ...

He'd done it. His plan had worked like a dream. He could go and see the England squad train at the City ground. He laughed out loud.

"Luke – one, Mum – nil!" he said, and went to get ready.

# Chapter 3
# A Near Thing

Luke took a long time to pick his clothes. He put on his favourite football shirt – the Spurs one with a number 10 on the back. He pulled on his football socks, then his jeans, and he tucked the bottoms of his jeans into his socks. Last of all, he put on his best trainers and did them up nice and tight.

He picked up his football boots, too – just in case he might need them – and went downstairs and into the kitchen. Luke hadn't

remembered. What about his front door key? What if he came back and couldn't get in? The thought made him go all hot and sweaty. He nipped back inside, picked up his key from the hall table and stepped out again.

It had been a near thing. But as he shut the door with the key firmly in his hand now, he couldn't help laughing to himself. Today was going to be a dream.

Luke pulled his hood tightly around his face – partly to keep the rain out, but also to make sure none of the neighbours saw him. He walked quickly along the street, sticking close to the hedges and garden walls. The bus arrived at the corner just as he got there. That was a relief – he wouldn't have to risk standing around waiting.

Just in case, he'd got his story all ready. If someone stopped him and asked why he wasn't at school he was going to say he was late. And on the way back he'd say he was going home for lunch! It was really easy!

Luke sat right at the back of the bus, and huddled down. He looked out over the wet, empty streets. Everything seemed different, somehow. There was hardly anyone about. He saw one old lady and then a mum with a pram, both going to the shops.

And then Luke saw a policeman.

He ducked down as quickly as he could. Had the policeman seen him?

That was the trouble about playing truant – it was all a bit stressful.

You had to keep away from places where someone from school might spot you, or where someone might know who you were. And if a policeman saw you out while everyone else was at school, he might ask tricky questions.

Luke could feel his heart thumping. He thought his story about being late would fool anyone who stopped him. But he couldn't be sure, could he?

In fact Luke began to think that playing truant wasn't a very good idea after all. The last time he'd done it, he'd been so worried about getting caught that he hadn't dared step outside the door. He'd ended up hanging around at home, dead bored. At least today he did have somewhere to go – and a chance to see something really exciting.

Luke sat up and peeped out of the window. He couldn't see the policeman any more – but he could see that he was nearly at the City ground. The main stand was in front of him, looming against the sky.

Most likely the England squad were inside it already. Luke jumped up from his seat, then sprang off the bus as soon as the doors opened. He made for the side entrance Jamie had told him to use. The players' entrance ...

"And it's Luke Bennett racing up the wing ..." he began to say to himself as he ran into the ground. What a day it would be!

# Chapter 4
## At the Ground

For a terrible moment Luke thought Jamie had been having him on. The ground looked totally empty, and he couldn't hear a sound. But as he walked down the touchline he began to hear shouting in the distance. He looked up, into one of the stands across from him, and saw some figures running up and down the terraces. A voice floated across the pitch, and an echo went round the ground.

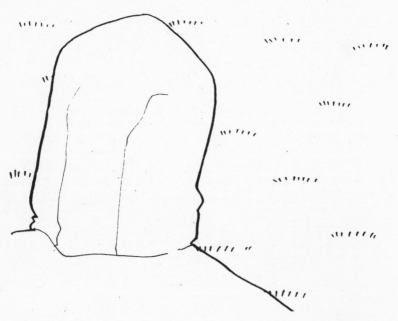

"Put some welly into it, John ... it's no good unless it hurts! Get those knees up, Wayne. Come on, Steve, let's see some real effort ..."

They were all there – the full England squad – and it looked as if they were being worked really hard by the assistant coach, Jimmy Taylor. Luke knew the professionals always started their training with some loosening up and some fitness exercises, perhaps even a run. But this looked like torture. Jimmy Taylor had them all running up the steep terraces to the top and back down again – and then right back up again.

Luke walked along the touchline and peered into the stand. It was in shadow, so he couldn't see much, and the sky was dark with rain clouds, which didn't make it any easier. But he could make out some faces he knew even from where he was, faces he'd only ever seen on TV before. And yes, there was Steve Browning …

"Come on, Steve!" Jimmy Taylor's voice boomed across the ground.

Steve Browning put on a sprint, but soon slowed down.

"Hey, Luke! You made it then! You escaped!"

Jamie was jogging down the touchline towards him.

"Yeah, I'm ill," Luke laughed. "My mum thinks I'm dying!"

Jamie laughed too. "What will she do if she finds out? Won't she give you a really hard time?"

"She's not going to find out, is she?" said Luke. "At least, I hope not. If she did she'd ban me from football for life."

They started to walk up the touchline. Luke could see a group of men standing near the corner of the pitch up at the other end. He knew who one of them was. Bill Mann – manager of the England team!

Luke couldn't really believe it. He'd seen Bill Mann on the TV and in the newspapers, and now here he was, in the flesh, real. Luke suddenly worked out that the men around him must be journalists. They were asking lots of questions. Every time Bill Mann said anything they wrote it down fast in their notebooks. A few of them were photographers – Luke could see that from the cameras they had slung all over them.

Jamie's dad was there too. He saw Luke and Jamie, and called them over. "Luke, Jamie," he said, "meet Bill Mann, manager of the next World Champions."

Bill Mann laughed.

"Nice of you to think so," he said. "We'll do our best, anyway." He turned to the two boys and held out his hand. Jamie shook hands first, and then it was Luke's turn. The England manager gripped his hand. Luke could hardly believe all this was really happening to him!

# Chapter 5
# A Tough Game

"You a footballer, son?" Bill Mann asked. He'd turned round to have a proper chat with Luke.

"Er ... yes, sir, I mean, I play for the school team, Mr Mann, sir." Luke could feel everyone looking at him, and his cheeks burning red. It was magic – he was talking to the England Manager.

"Football's the greatest sport in the world," Mr Mann was saying. "Do you want to be a professional one day?"

Luke grinned. "Definitely, sir."

"Keep at it, then, son. Keep at it." Mr Mann turned to look at his players who were making their way on to the pitch. Then he turned back to Luke and smiled again.

"Did the school give you the day off to come and watch? Pick up a few ideas for the school team, maybe?"

Luke could feel himself blush even more deeply.

"Er ... well, yes, but, well ... not exactly ..." He didn't know what to say. But his mouth was open and he had to say something, even if it did all come out sounding like rubbish.

Bill Mann's smile vanished. He started to wag his finger very slowly at Luke.

"Naughty, naughty ... you haven't skived off from school, have you?" he said.

"Well ..." Luke didn't finish.

"I'll give you a bit of advice, son, and if I were you, it's advice I'd listen to. Football's a tough game. What happens if you don't make it as a professional? Amateur teams are full of good players who weren't good enough to make it in the league. If you don't make it, you'll need something to fall back on, won't you?"

"Yes, sir, I mean, Mr Mann," Luke stuttered.

"That's right. You'll need some exams. You keep up your school work. It's hard enough getting a job of any sort these days," Mr Mann was looking right at Luke.

Luke felt that he was blushing from the roots of his hair to the ends of his toes. He didn't know where to look. Everyone seemed to be staring at him – and at Jamie too. He thought that Mr Mann would get on very well with his mum. But then Bill Mann laughed again.

"Don't take it too badly, son. One day won't make that much of a difference, so long as it is only one day, mind. And so long as you promise me you'll make a special effort at school from now on."

"Oh I will, Mr Mann, I will," Luke promised.

Bill Mann turned to the journalists. "I used to have the odd day off myself to go and watch Newcastle United train when I was a lad. My mum nearly killed me when she found out, though. She still thinks I should have worked harder at school and forgotten

about football!" Everyone else laughed now too.

"Well, this won't do," Bill Mann went. "I'd better make sure the lads are working." He turned to Luke and Jamie again. "Enjoy your day, boys – and remember what I've said!"

He walked on to the pitch.

And Luke did enjoy his day, every second of it. Jamie had brought a ball along. While the squad was finishing off its fitness training and exercises, he and Luke had a kick-about at the other end of the pitch. But their eyes kept drifting towards their heroes. At last, Luke and Jamie saw that the squad was going to practise some set-piece moves, and they ran round to watch.

Luke and Jamie stood a few yards to one side of the goal. The England goalie Peter Sharpe was already standing on the line.

"Hey up, lads, I wouldn't stand there when that Steve Browning's shooting," he said. "You'd be safer standing in the middle of the goal."

Luke and Jamie laughed, and they laughed even more when they heard the name Steve Browning called Peter Sharpe. For Luke it was paradise. He was here with his heroes and they were talking and joking with him!

It was great watching the free-kick moves too. They promised Peter Sharpe and the other players that they wouldn't say a word to the French team about England's special plans. Not before the big game. Luke almost felt part of the England squad. He spent most of the morning dreaming about his favourite fantasy – the one about pulling on an England shirt and playing in the World Cup Final.

He could almost feel the ball at his feet, feel the power in his legs as he volleyed the winning goal into the net from 35 yards. He could feel himself punching the sky and turning round so as to get the hugs and shouts of his team mates and the wild cheers of the crowd ...

# Chapter 6
# Dream Goal

"Hey, you two! Wanna game?"

Luke looked at Jamie, and Jamie looked at Luke. Then they both looked towards Steve Browning, who was running towards them from the little group of players in the middle of the pitch.

"Well, do you want a game or not? We're two short for a full side and we need a couple of nifty players." He was grinning.

Luke looked at Jamie again – and Jamie looked at Luke.

"Yeah!" they both shouted.

And then they were on the pitch, trotting towards the centre spot, towards Luke's favourite dream. Bill Mann smiled at them both, then looked around at all the players.

"Well, you lot, these two are my secret weapon. They're a couple of young players I've been bringing along in secret, and they're going to give you hell. Remember, they're after your places." He winked at Luke and Jamie. Luke couldn't believe it was really happening.

Steve Browning put him in mid-field, on the right-hand side, and Jamie on the left. He laughed and joked with the boys and told them there was no way they'd lose today with Sharpey in goal ... And they were kicking off. Luke was actually playing in a training match with the England squad, and on the same team as his hero, Steve Browning!

It was all like a beautiful dream while he was playing. Everything he did went right. He passed well, ran off the ball well, even tackled well, even if he did know none of the squad were trying hard. There was lots of laughing and joking. Danny Thomson, the Aston Villa midfielder, went flying every time he was on the ball and Luke went near him.

"Ref! That kid's a killer! He's after me all the time!" he moaned.

The ref was, of course, Bill Mann, who was also playing up front for the other team. He was panting a bit but he seemed to be having a lot of fun. And what made it all the better for Luke was that Bill Mann kept giving him advice.

"Easy, take it easy now son, head up, look for a spare man now!" he shouted.

And when Luke made a good pass, Bill Mann would run past and tell him he was playing well. Jamie wasn't having a bad game either.

They were only playing 15 minutes each way, and after they'd changed ends, Luke had the feeling he always had when he was in a match he was enjoying – he didn't want it to end. He would have been happy to play on for days, weeks, months. He dreaded the sound of the final whistle.

He knew it couldn't be far away when he picked up the ball from Steve Browning just inside the other half. Danny Thomson laid back from him, and he could hear other members of the team calling for the ball in space. Jamie was to his left, moving towards the area, so he let him have it. Jamie put it straight on to Steve Browning who took it on a speed run to the corner flag – just like in Luke's favourite fantasy!

Luke moved into the area, calling for the ball. Danny Thomson, a grin still on his face – but with an eye for the ball, just like the pro he was – drifted in with him. Steve Browning checked his run near the corner flag, beat his marker, and looked up to see where everyone was.

Luke had his arm up, and he was calling for the ball. He looked at Peter Sharpe, who was on his goal line. The keeper smiled at him, and then looked out at Steve Browning. Luke saw Steve Browning hit the cross over, and then his eyes went back to the ball. He watched it curve over the heads of the defenders. It was coming towards him ...

And then he was running, his eyes still fixed firmly on that ball. Everything seemed to go into silent slow motion, and there was nothing else in the world but Luke and that ball. He was running faster and faster, he felt both feet leave the ground, he felt, rather than saw, where the ball was ... his head connected with it with a THUD! and then he slid over in the goal mouth mud and skidded to a stop just near Peter Sharpe.

The world clicked back into being normal again. Luke heard shouts, cheering.

He looked up and the net was still rippling from where the ball had slid down it and into the back of the goal. He'd scored with a beautiful diving header.

He'd scored a goal against the England keeper.

ONE NIL!

# Chapter 7
# Action Replay

"Great goal, son, great goal!"

It was Steve Browning who helped Luke up off the ground and patted him so hard on the back that he nearly fell over again.

"You doing anything next Wednesday night? We need a striker," Steve Browning said.

He had his arm round Luke as they walked back to the centre spot. All the other players called out and clapped, and Bill Mann blew three long, loud blasts on his whistle for the end of the game.

"Good goal, son," he said to Luke, then shouted at Peter Sharpe. "And where were you, Sharpey? You should have taken out the cross!"

"It was way too good for him," said Steve Browning.

"It wasn't the cross, boss – that was rubbish. Any chance of dropping Browning and playing the lad instead?" asked Peter Sharpe. Everyone laughed and whistled.

"If I'm out, you're out," shouted Steve Browning – and chased Peter Sharpe down the players' tunnel.

Luke heard all this but he wasn't really listening. He was stuck in an action replay of his goal. He felt he was walking about ten feet above the ground. And he kept on feeling that way until he saw some of the players coming out of their dressing room a bit later to get in their cars and drive off. Bill Mann said he could keep the ball he'd scored with. The players had washed it off and dried it for him so that the squad could sign it. They'd done the same for Jamie with another ball.

All the players had a word for him as they signed the ball, and both Luke and Jamie wished them luck for the match on Wednesday. One by one the cars started to drive away from the car park, until there was only Bill Mann and a couple of the journalists left.

"Can you sign it for me too, Mr Mann?" Luke asked.

"Sure, son." Mr Mann pulled out an expensive looking pen and found an empty space on the ball. "Now, you remember what I said about your school work. But why don't you come down to one of City's trials in a season or two? They've got a good academy. You could do worse."

And then he got in his car and drove away.

"Hey Jamie, it's been a great day," said Luke.

"Too right," said Jamie. "You've done yourself some favours there, Luke. You'll be playing for England next."

"You didn't play too badly yourself," said Luke.

Luke coughed, and coughed again. His throat was beginning to feel a little tickly, and he felt a bit hot and woozy, too. But he didn't take much notice. He liked what Jamie had said, but he couldn't tell him about his secret hope – that Bill Mann would remember him.

"Yeah, well, see you," said Luke and turned to go home.

Luke sat at the back of the bus home, and looked out at the empty streets. It was just after twelve o'clock and in only a few hours the streets would start filling up again with kids coming home from school. All they'd had was a really boring day, the same as any other. But he had something to remember. The only pity was that it was over, though he'd definitely find out about the City trials.

The other problem was that he couldn't talk about his day to anyone, at least not to his mum or dad. Dad would be really interested, over the moon, probably, if he knew. But they'd murder him if they found out he'd been skiving off school. He'd have to hide the football he'd got as well, at least until he could think of a good excuse for having it. Maybe he'd say Jamie's dad had got it for him. That was it – perfect!

Luke let himself into the still, empty house. He made some toast and had a glass of milk. His throat felt more than a bit tickly now. It felt sore and he was coughing a lot. He was hotter too, and shivery.

He went upstairs and got undressed. He stuffed his muddy clothes in a bag and shoved them under his bed, along with the ball the squad had given him. Then he got into bed. He lay stuck in an action replay of his goal. It had been so perfect – the curving flight of the ball, the way his head had made contact with it as he jumped up ... He fell asleep with a huge smile on his face.

# Chapter 8
# Big Trouble

Luke didn't remember much more of the afternoon. He didn't remember his sister coming home and peering at him. He didn't remember his mum coming in and putting her hand on his head again but for a second her ring felt nice and cool on his face. He didn't remember her fussing over him, and he didn't know that she phoned the doctor, who promised to come in the morning.

He woke for a few minutes, late in the evening, and knew that he was really ill. But it didn't seem to matter. He knew he'd done something very good, but he couldn't remember what it was. Then he fell asleep again.

When he woke the next morning, he felt a little better, but his throat was still sore and it hurt when he coughed. But it didn't seem to matter. He could remember the day before, and the thought of his goal made him smile. He could hear noise from the kitchen, so everyone else was up and about. He knew he wouldn't be able to go to school today. He smiled. It wasn't a skive, either, this time.

Just as he was drifting off into an action replay of his goal again, his bedroom door opened. His sister poked her head round.

"Who's in big trouble, then?" she said, and laughed.

"What?" he croaked. Too late. His sister had gone. Then he heard footsteps coming up the stairs and along the landing towards his door. It opened, and his mum came in, holding the newspaper.

"Well, how's our poor sick boy this morning?" she said.

Luke tried a weak smile. Mum was looking a bit grim.

"Er ... I think I feel a bit better," he said.

"I'm glad," said Mum. She was smiling now, but it wasn't a real smile. It looked nasty. Luke had seen one like it before. His mum smiled like that just before a grade A, number one, total telling off. "I thought you might like to read the paper," Mum went on. "I've brought it up for you."

His mum tossed it at him. Luke looked at her, puzzled.

"Open it, then," she said. "The sports pages."

Luke did as he was told. Then he gulped hard and it hurt his throat. There, right in front of his eyes, in the paper for all to see, was a picture of him standing next to Bill Mann. One of those photographers must have taken it yesterday! There was a headline under the photo, too. "Mann plans for the future." There was also a little story about how "two schoolboys" had been watching England train at City's ground, and one of them had put a goal past Peter Sharpe in a training match. The journalist had written at the end of the story: "... and let's hope Sharpey was only messing about when he got beaten by a kid."

It was a killer, really. At any other time he would have been sky-high with pride. Not only had he played with the England squad

and scored a goal – he'd got his picture in the paper! But he was in trouble instead.

Big trouble. He opened his mouth to say something. Mum held up her hand.

"Don't bother to say anything," she muttered. "I only hope for your sake that they'll be OK about this at school when they see it – and, trust me, they will see this."

Luke hadn't thought of that. He felt even worse.

"Me and your dad were gobsmacked when we saw it," Mum went on. "You are never to lie to me like that again. We're the ones who get taken to court if you skive off, you know. If you ever do it again, I'll ... I'll ..."

Luke's mum sat on the bed, and for a moment, he thought she was going to cry. But she looked up and shook her head – then she smiled.

"You should have heard your dad," she said at last.

"Er ... was he really angry?" said Luke. Dad had a bit of a temper.

"Angry?" his mum said. "He didn't know where to put himself for pride. But he's still going to give you a good telling off when you're feeling better."

"So you do believe I'm ill today?" said Luke.

His mum looked at him hard.

"I believe you," she said. "Thousands wouldn't."

Luke smiled at her. She stood up and went to the door. She stopped, then turned to look at him once more.

"And your punishment will be ..." she said and waited a moment. She went on. "No pocket money – and no playing football outside school ... for a month."

"A whole month!" Luke croaked. "But Mum, that's just not fair!"

It was too late. The door was shut behind her. Then he heard her laugh, and her last words on the subject floating up the stairs.

"Mum – one ... son – nil."

Barrington Stoke would like to thank all its readers for commenting on the manuscript before publication and in particular:

Fiona Devereux
Chloe Ford-Welman
Fraser Gibbs
Marina Hacking
Lizzie Hill
Kate Hodgson
Katharina
June McCleave
Louise M.D.
Brian O'Neill
May O'Neill
Kate Walling

## Become a Consultant!

Would you like to give us feedback on our titles before they are published? Contact us at the email address below – we'd love to hear from you!

info@barringtonstoke.co.uk
www.barringtonstoke.co.uk